Gary Paulsen

Culpepper's Cannon

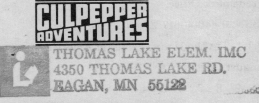

A YEARLING BOOK

Published by
Dell Publishing
a division of
Bantam Doubleday Dell Publishing Group, Inc.
1540 Broadway
New York, New York 10036

ISBN: 0-440-40617-X

Printed in the United States of America

August 1992

10   9   8   7   6   5   4

OPM

Chapter·1

Duncan—Dunc—Culpepper sat on the ground with his back against the one good wheel of the cannon that stood in front of the county courthouse. He was watching Amos Binder, his best friend—from the day they were born to the day they died, his best friend for life. Amos was sitting on the ground in front of him and rubbing his forehead.

"What did you do this time?" Dunc asked.

"I bumped my head."

"I can see that. What I meant was, what did you do to bump your head?"

1

"I was riding my bike down Cross Street, and I saw Melissa. She saw me and waved."

"She waved at you?"

"I swear. If my mother was dead, I'd swear on her grave. She waved at me."

Dunc didn't believe him. Maybe she looked as if she had waved, maybe she was trying to frighten a mosquito away and Amos thought she had waved, but Melissa Hansen would not have waved. Amos had been in love with Melissa for life—from the day he was born to the day he died, in love with her for life. Melissa Hansen didn't even know Amos existed, probably never would know, and probably never would care.

"So what happened?" he asked.

"Well, I turned to wave back, trying to be real cool, but when I turned I forgot I was riding my bike, and I turned the handlebars with me. I hit the curb and bounced across the street right into the bed of a pickup. I was going so fast, I flew off my bike over the bed and ran my face into the back of the cab."

"Are you all right?"

"I'm fine. I just hope the owner of the pickup doesn't want me to pay for it."

"Why, did he see you?"

"He didn't have to. He'll be able to recognize me from the face imprint in the back of his cab." He rubbed his forehead again.

Dunc stood up and stretched. It was early March and the first warm Saturday of the year. He and Amos were going to go to the library, but as soon as they stepped outside, they had both realized that the sun was too warm to spend the afternoon there. Amos stretched and smiled at the sun on his face.

"So what are you going to write your paper on?" Dunc asked. Amos had Mr. Trasky for American history. Mr. Trasky loved assigning papers. Students hated getting Mr. Trasky.

"I don't know. I just don't want to think about it. I hate writing papers." Amos quit rubbing his forehead and buried his face in his hands.

"What's it have to be about?"

"The Civil War. I hate the Civil War."

"Why?"

"Because I can never remember anything about it. It goes through my head like water through a funnel."

"For a paper on the Civil War, we're at the perfect place. This cannon was in the Civil War."

Amos looked up. "You mean that thing is real? I always thought it was made out of plaster of Paris or something. You know, a decoration."

"Don't you ever read?"

"Sure I read. I just finished a book about how to attract girls. It gave me some pointers for Melissa. You see, if I—"

"I mean this plaque." He pointed with his thumb toward the other side of the cannon. "Haven't you ever read this plaque about the cannon?"

"No."

"Come here." Dunc stood and waited for Amos to climb groaning to his feet. He was still sore from his adventure with the pickup. Dunc led him to the other side of the cannon.

The wooden wheel was broken on that side, and a concrete block with a plaque on it supported the axle. " 'This cannon was part of the arsenal during the battle between the *Merrimack* and the *Monitor*, March 9, 1862,' " Dunc read aloud. " 'Dedicated in memory of the men who served there.' "

"Wow," Amos said. "And I always thought it was a fake."

"It isn't. You should read more."

Amos leaned over and looked at the wooden axle that ran under the cannon. "I wonder what happened to its wheel?" he asked.

"I don't know."

Amos's face brightened up. He got that look that came when he found an idea that was great. Or at least an idea that he thought was great. "Hey, do you suppose I could do my paper on this cannon?"

"On this cannon?"

"Yeah, you know, its history. Like how it broke its wheel."

"I don't know. Where would you find something like that out?"

"I don't know." The brightness left his

face, and he looked like he usually looked again.

Dunc looked at him and then at the cannon. He wanted to help Amos, to brighten him up again. After all, they were best friends for life.

"Why don't you write your paper about cannons? You know, all cannons. You could write about how the were made and how they were used and what kind of cannonballs they fired. You could use this one as an example."

It worked. When Amos looked up, his face was bright again. "I could do that, couldn't I?" He reached out and touched the cannon with his hand. "I could write about all that and other things, too, like the tactics used with them. Old Trasky would like that, wouldn't he?" He walked around the cannon, examining it. Dunc followed him. On the other side was a stack of cannonballs.

"Say," Amos said. "How much do you suppose one of these things weighs?" He reached over and tried to pick one of them up. It wouldn't budge. He planted his feet more firmly and put all the muscles in his back and legs into it. It still wouldn't budge.

"I've never seen anything so little and so heavy in my whole life," he said.

Dunc shook his head. "It's cemented down, you dummy."

Amos examined the cannonball and saw the mortar holding it to the balls it was stacked on. He looked up sheepishly. "Gee, I guess you're right. Why do you suppose they do that?"

"Probably to keep people from blowing up McPhereson's department store," Dunc said. McPhereson's was across the street.

"I guess you're right." He walked back to the front of the cannon and tried to stuff his fist in the end of the barrel. "Do you suppose this thing would still work? Can it work with a broken wheel? I wonder—hey, check this out."

"What's the matter?"

Amos looked at Dunc. His eyes flashed with excitement. "There's something in here."

Chapter·2

Dunc watched Amos dangling from the cannon, his forearm crammed down the barrel. "What is it?" he asked.

"I don't know." Amos was trying to stick his arm farther down the barrel.

"Be careful," Dunc said. "If your fist gets stuck, I might have to use a cannonball to blow it out. You could end up across the street at McPhereson's."

"Funny."

"If whatever it is is furry and moves by itself, you'd better leave it alone. I saw on the news last night that a great fanged wombat had escaped from the zoo."

"A great fanged wombat?"

"It's the nastiest animal I could come up with on such short notice."

"Oh, another funny. I almost believed you." Amos began to carefully pull his arm back out of the barrel. "I've got it. It's a piece of paper." He had his arm out now, and his sleeve was covered with dirt and rust. A yellowed piece of paper was in his hand. He tried to unfold it, and a corner broke off in his fingers. The wind grabbed at the corner and carried it away.

Dunc took the paper from him. "Be careful—you don't want to ruin it." They sat down on the lawn.

"What do you suppose it is?" Amos asked.

"I don't know yet." Dunc unfolded it carefully. Little bits and pieces broke off and blew away in the breeze. "There's writing on it."

"What's it say?"

"I'm not sure. It's pretty faded." They both leaned over it. The writing was thin and gray and just barely visible.

"Maybe it tells where some money is,"

Amos said, "or maybe it describes a murderer. Maybe—"

"Shush. Let me read this." Dunc bent over the paper farther until his nose was almost touching it. " 'Look out for Bremish,' " he read aloud. " 'He'll kill us if he gets a chance. The time portal is at the southwest corner of the plaza. When you go through, don't forget "gazebo." I think you only get one chance, and if it closes on you, you're stuck here forever.' " He looked up at Amos. "That's it."

"Time portal?"

"That's what it says."

"I wonder what it means?"

"A time portal might be like a hole in time."

"A time hole?"

"Yeah."

"That's crazy. This must be some kind of a joke."

"I don't know," Dunc said. "This paper's awfully old. When this was written, they probably didn't know about time portals."

"They must have. The guy who wrote this did, anyway."

"Maybe that's because the guy who wrote this came from the future."

"No way. I don't believe it." Amos rubbed his forehead again. "Is it signed?"

Dunc looked down at the paper. "There's a *D*, but the rest of the signature was on the corner you broke off."

"Who's Bremish?"

"You got me."

"Why do you suppose he was after whoever wrote the note?"

"I don't know. Maybe they stole something from him. Maybe they stole something valuable."

"What do you suppose it was?"

"I don't know."

Amos rubbed his forehead thoughtfully. "If there is a time hole, where do you suppose it is? Where was this plaza?"

Dunc looked up at Amos. His eyes were gleaming. "There's only one way to find out."

Amos leaned back away from Dunc. "You've got that look," he said.

"What look?"

12

"Come on, Dunc, don't do this to me. I've got to write a paper."

"It won't take long. We'll just go down to the library and find out where this plaza was, then we'll go to whatever is there now. It'll only take a couple of minutes."

"Then you do it yourself. I've got to write a paper."

"Maybe what they took from Bremish will still be at the plaza. Maybe it will help you with your paper."

"I don't care. Every time we do something like this, I get into trouble."

"Maybe it's something valuable. Maybe it's treasure. There's no better way to impress a girl than with treasure."

Amos looked at him, suddenly interested. "Really?"

"Really." Dunc leaned back and studied Amos carefully, the way a cobra might study a bird just before it struck. "I wonder what kind of treasure a girl like Melissa would be impressed by?"

But it was overkill. Amos was already on his feet. "What are you waiting for?" he asked. "Let's go find this plaza."

Chapter · 3

"No. Absolutely not. I will not go in there."
Amos was standing in front of La Petite, a
women's clothing store. He looked at Dunc.

"Come on, Amos," Dunc said. "The old
maps at the library said this is where the
southwest corner of the plaza was. We have
to go in there."

"I thought it said southeast. If it said
southeast, maybe it's in the sporting goods
store across the street."

"No. It was southwest. You can never remember directions. We have to go in here."

"No, we don't. This is all somebody's idea
of a sick joke. I'm not going in there."

"Why not? What's so bad about a women's clothing store?"

"This isn't just a women's clothing store. This is Melissa's favorite women's clothing store. What if she sees me in there? She'll think I'm weird or something."

"Why is that weird?"

"A guy buying women's clothing isn't weird?"

"Look, if she sees you, just tell her you're buying something for your mother."

"No."

"Then tell her you're buying something for her."

"Why would I be buying something for her?"

"Tell her you thought it was her birthday, and you're getting her a sweater. She'll like that."

Amos looked through the front window of the store. An older woman was looking at stockings, and a sales clerk was helping her. He looked back at Dunc. "You really think so?"

"Do you know anyone who isn't impressed by presents?"

"You might be right, but I can't afford a sweater."

"Buy it with the treasure we find."

Amos looked through the window again and was silent for a moment. "All right. But just a couple of minutes. If we don't find this hole right away, we're leaving."

"Portal. The word is *portal*."

"I like *hole*. It's more descriptive. And if we don't find it right away, we're leaving."

"All right." Dunc held the door open, and Amos went in in front of him.

The air in the store was air-conditioned cool and had a thick, scented smell that caught in Amos's throat. He looked around the store. There were dresses and skirts and blouses and underthings he felt embarrassed looking at. He didn't see any holes. "Nothing," he said. "Let's go."

"Not yet," Dunc said. "It should be in the back corner. Let's go have a look."

Dunc led Amos to the back of the store. There was a rack of women's jeans and a table covered with thick sweaters. Dunc pointed. "There," he said. "It has to be in there."

"No. If it's in there, I want to forget the whole thing." Dunc was pointing at a women's changing room.

"We have to," Dunc said. "We've come this far." He looked around the store. When he looked back at him, Amos could see that gleam in his eye again. "You're going to have to try something on."

"Me? Why me?"

"Because you look more like someone who would try on women's clothing than I do."

Amos looked at Dunc. "What's that supposed to mean?"

"I don't mean anything bad. I mean you look more sensitive, like you would go to greater lengths to make sure a sweater fit a girl right before you bought it. Melissa is closer to your size than she is to mine."

"Oh. That's what I thought you meant." He sighed deeply. "All right, I'll do it, but don't let anyone see me."

"I won't." Dunc tried to open the dressing-room door. It was locked. "We'll have to get help from the clerk. Grab a sweater. Make sure it's one Melissa would like."

Amos took a pink one, then decided against it. He reached for a thick green one with a collar and followed Dunc up to the checkout counter.

The clerk had finished with the older woman and was standing at the counter writing something on a piece of paper. When Dunc and Amos approached him he looked up. He was a tall, thin man with a name tag that said *Ramone* and a nose that hooked down almost to his chin. His hair was so heavily hairsprayed, it looked hard enough to play a good game of basketball on.

"Can I help you?" His voice was high and whiny, and when he spoke, his Adam's apple jumped up at least two inches.

"My friend here would like to try on this sweater," Dunc said.

"Your friend would like to try on this sweater?" Ramone looked coldly at Amos, and Amos felt his face turn red. "Why would your friend like to try on a women's sweater?"

"It's a gift," Dunc said.

"A gift for a girl?" Ramone asked.

19

"Of course it's for a girl," Amos said.

"Just checking." Ramone chuckled. When he chuckled, his Adam's apple moved up and down so violently, Amos thought it would bruise the bottom of his chin. "Let me get the key." He reached into a drawer and took out a key on the end of a large slab of wood. He led them back through the store toward the dressing room.

"There you are," Ramone said, unlocking the door. "I trust you won't be needing any help?"

"I don't think so," Amos said.

"Good." Ramone chuckled again. He walked back toward the checkout counter, straightening the racks of dresses as he went. Dunc and Amos went into the dressing room.

The room was small, with a single bulb overhead and three walls covered with mirrors. There was no sign of a hole or anything that might even resemble one.

"So do we have everything?" Dunc asked.

"Everything for what?"

"Time travel."

"Do you know what we need to travel through time?"

"No."

"Then why are you asking such a stupid question?" Amos was getting mad about the whole situation. "The only thing I brought was a notebook, and I only brought that because you said I'd need it."

"Notes for your paper."

"Right. Notes for my paper." Amos looked at Dunc. "So now what do we do?"

"It has to be here. There's no other place it could be."

"Well, I don't see anything."

"Of course not. Do you think if you could see it people wouldn't know about it?"

"So what do we do?"

"I don't know." Dunc stood with his hands on his hips. He chewed on his lower lip thoughtfully.

"You know, this isn't a bad-looking sweater," Amos said. "I wonder if Melissa would like it. Here, hang on to this." He handed his notebook to Dunc and started to pull his sweatshirt off over his head.

"What are you doing?"

"Trying on this sweater. You said I was closer to Melissa's size than you were."

"We didn't come in here to try on sweaters."

"Well, we might as well do something useful."

Dunc ignored him. "There must be something we're missing."

Amos had his shirt pulled halfway over his head. "Wasn't there something about a gazelle?"

"No, *gazelle* wasn't the word. What was it?" He reached into his back pocket for the paper. It was in considerably worse condition than it had been before.

"Hey, can you help me with this?" Amos still had his sweatshirt halfway over his head. He was having difficulty taking it off in the small confines of the room.

" 'Look out for Bremish. He'll kill us if he gets a chance,' " Dunc read, ignoring Amos again. " 'The time portal is at the southwest corner of the plaza. When you go through, don't forget "gazebo"—' "

When he said the word *gazebo,* the mirror on the right-hand wall began to throb with a glowing yellow light. It made a sound like a heart pumping and it pulsated three times, stopped, and pulsated three times again.

"Do you see that?" Dunc almost yelled. "Do you see that?"

"See what?" Amos's sweatshirt was still over his head. He couldn't see anything.

"It's here, it's right here!" Dunc reached out to touch the mirror. His hand went through it as if nothing were there. A moment later, he stepped through and was gone. The pulsating light and the sound of the heart stopped. The mirror was a mirror again.

"Come on, Dunc, help me with this shirt. And quit ignoring me. What do you mean it's here? And what does gazebo have to do with anything?" At the word *gazebo,* the heart sound started again, and the yellow light started pulsating. It had only two beats this time, but Amos couldn't see that.

"Come on, Dunc, help me with this shirt." He started banging against the walls to find Dunc. When he tried moving to the right, he found there wasn't a wall there. A moment later, the mirror was just a mirror and the dressing room was empty again.

Chapter · 4

Amos's sweatshirt was still over his head. He was lying on the floor, and the floor appeared to be covered with gravel. "Don't they ever clean this place?" he said out loud. He tried to sit up, but his sense of balance was off and he fell over again. He stayed on the floor, breathing heavily, until his head stopped spinning.

As soon as his mind cleared, he sat up and pulled his sweatshirt back down. Immediately he sensed that somehow he wasn't where he was supposed to be. For one thing, the store wasn't there anymore, and the floor wasn't dirty because the floor wasn't there anymore, either. The floor had turned into a gravel courtyard, and the store had turned into a large open area with stone buildings on all four sides and a tall stone pillar right in the middle. He looked up and saw stars shining down. He looked around him and saw horses and men in gray uniforms and cannons, cannons everywhere. Dunc wasn't there, either. Dunc got him into this mess, and when Dunc got him into a mess, Dunc was supposed to be there to get him out. Dunc wasn't anywhere to be seen.

"Dunc, where are you?"

No one answered. Men were rushing about, some with beards and some with long moustaches and some not old enough to have either, but none of them were Dunc and none of them paid him any more attention than a quick, curious glance. He stood up, a little wobbly at first.

"Dunc, where are you?"

Again no one answered. He started walking around the courtyard, looking at the faces of the men busy at work, trying to find one that he recognized. He didn't. He began to feel panic tighten up his chest.

"Dunc, where are you? Dunc!"

"Quit your shouting, boy." Amos looked behind him. Two men were standing against the wall of a dry goods store watching him. One was tall with a pot belly, and the other was short, and when he moved, his movements were quick, like a bird's. "Get over here, boy, out of the way." Amos obeyed.

"Boy, what are you dressed so funny for?" the tall one said. Amos looked down at his clothes. He was still wearing his favorite sweatshirt, a pair of blue jeans, and his white cross trainers with the orange stripes down the sides. He didn't think he was dressed funny at all.

"I—I—"

"What's your name, boy?" the tall one asked.

"Amos. Amos Binder."

"Good name," the tall one said. "A good southern name."

"Good southern name," the little one echoed.

"Where am I?" Amos asked.

"Where are you?" The tall one laughed and nudged the little one with his elbow. "He asked where he was."

"Where he was," the little one repeated, giggling.

"Well?" Amos was getting impatient.

The tall one eyed Amos suspiciously. "You don't know where you are?" he asked.

"I'm not sure."

"Where are you from, boy?"

"From?" the little one repeated.

"I'm from here," Amos said, "I guess."

The tall one spat on the ground. "I've lived here all my life, and I've never seen you. How come I've never seen you?"

"Seen you?" the little one said, eyeing Amos as suspiciously as the tall one did.

Amos thought for a moment. "Well, I'm from here, but I'm not from here. Do you know what I mean?"

"No," the tall one said. He rubbed his chin. The little one did, too. "If you're from around here, then you should know what happened here today. What happened here today?"

"Today?" the little one asked. They were both eyeing him and rubbing their chins.

Amos thought. He had never been much good at American history. He looked around and saw the men in their gray uniforms and the cannons. He had to assume he was in the Civil War. He hated the Civil War. The Civil War was like water through a funnel to him—he couldn't remember anything about it.

The two men were still watching him, even more suspicious than before, and Amos saw that he would have to think fast. He didn't know what to say. He took a shot in the dark.

"A battle was fought here." He tried to sound as if he know what he was talking about. He didn't think he succeeded.

The tall one smiled and nodded his head proudly. He nudged the little one. "I told you he knew."

"He knew," the little one said. He tried to nod his head proudly, too, but his movements were too jerky for that. His head vibrated like a ringing bell.

"A battle, a great battle," the tall one

said. "Fought by our valiant ship, the *Virginia*. She went out and whipped on those Yankees like a stepmother whips a wayward child. It was a grand thing to see. Long live the South!" He stood up straight and saluted, beaming proudly.

"The South!" the little one said. He mimicked his friend. His head was still vibrating. After a respectful silence, they both slumped against the wall again.

Amos couldn't believe his luck. The *Virginia* was one of the few things he remembered about the Civil War, one of the few things that had stayed in the funnel. It was originally named the *Merrimack*. The South had renamed it and armed it with iron plates, the first ship to have armor. She sank several Union wooden ships the day before she met the Union's armored ship, named the *Monitor*. This must be the day before.

"It was a grand thing to see, wasn't it?" Amos said confidently. "A really grand thing to see on a March 8, 1862." The *Merrimack* had fought the *Monitor* on March ninth. Today had to be the eighth.

"A grand thing to see," the tall one repeated. Evidently Amos had gotten the date right.

The tall one leaned over again. "But I hear tell that the Yankees have a metal ship, too," he whispered. His eyes darted back and forth as if he expected to find someone eavesdropping.

"They do," Amos said. "It's called the *Monitor*. It will be here tomorrow."

"How do you know that?" The tall one was suspicious again, but Amos was too proud of the one bit of history he knew to notice it.

"Know that?" the little one repeated.

"Because today is March 8, 1862, and that makes tomorrow March ninth. The *Merrimack* and the *Monitor* fought each other on March ninth."

"Why are you talking like tomorrow's already happened?" the tall one asked. "And why did you call the good ship *Virginia* a stinking Yankee name like the *Merrimack*? Are you a spy?"

"A spy?" Amos asked. He realized he had overplayed his hand.

31

The tall one grabbed his shoulder. "You are a spy, aren't you? A spy!"

"A spy!" the little one shouted.

"Sergeant!" the tall one called. "We've caught ourselves a spy!"

"A spy!" the little one shouted again.

A big man the size of a small economy car turned his head and looked at them. He had a huge red handlebar moustache that made it look like his lip had burst into flame. "What's that?" he called.

"A spy! We've caught ourselves a spy!"

"A spy!" the little one said again.

Amos saw the sergeant start to walk toward him. He was so big that every time he took a step, Amos thought he could feel the ground tremble. He tried to shake himself free of the tall man, but he had a stronger grip than he looked like he should have had.

Before Amos could get away, the sergeant had a hold on his shoulder, and he quit struggling. He knew he would never get away from the sergeant. He knew he would never get away from a grip like that. It was like a vise.

"A spy, eh?" The sergeant's voice was as

strong as his grip was. He looked at Amos with startling blue eyes. "You're right," he said. "He's a spy."

"I'm not a spy," Amos protested.

"Right. That's what the other one said, too."

"The other one?" Amos asked. "There's another one?"

"There's another one," the sergeant said, "and he's dressed just like you."

Chapter · 5

"He's a spy, sir," the sergeant said. "He was talking about the *Virginia,* and he called it the Yankee name."

Amos was standing in a canvas tent in front of a captain of the Army of the Confederacy. The captain was an older man with a bald head. He had a fringe of white hair and gold-rimmed glasses with little round lenses. He sweated and continually dabbed at his forehead with a handkerchief.

"Did he now?" The captain leaned over his desk and looked at Amos. "And what do you have to say for yourself?"

"I'm not a spy," Amos said. "I live here."

"Well, fine," the captain said. "That should be easy to verify. We'll just talk to your mother."

Amos swallowed loudly. "Well, you can't do that."

"Why not?"

"Because she's not from here. Well, she is, but she isn't. She isn't *yet*." The captain stared at him blankly. "It's kind of hard to explain."

The captain left the question hanging in the air. He pointed at Amos's sweatshirt. "What is that?" he asked.

Amos looked down. He was wearing a sweatshirt that his parents had bought him when they visited Gettysburg National Military Park the year before. There was a picture of a cannon and a grave and two crossed flags, one the Union's and one the Confederacy's. He looked back up. He didn't know what to say.

"It's a shirt," he said.

"I can see that. What's it say on it?"

"Gettysburg, sir."

"That's what I thought it said." The captain dabbed at his forehead. "Sergeant Bremish."

Amos looked at the sergeant. "Your name is Bremish?"

"Yeah. So?" Amos looked at him but didn't say anything.

"Sergeant Bremish," the captain repeated, "have you ever heard of a Gettysburg?"

"I believe there's a town up north called that, sir."

"Where at?"

"Pennsylvania, I believe, sir."

"Yes, I thought so. Do you suppose this lad is from there?"

"Probably, sir."

"And that would make him a spy, wouldn't it?"

"Yes, sir."

"Yes, I thought so." The captain took off his glasses, tried to clean them with his sweaty handkerchief, and put them back on.

Amos swallowed again. "What do you do with spies?" he asked.

"Generally, we shoot them," the captain said. "Isn't that what we do, Sergeant?"

"Yes, sir."

"Yes, I thought that's what we did with them." The captain dabbed at his forehead with his handkerchief.

"I'm not a spy, I swear," Amos said. "Cross my heart, hope to die, stick a needle in my eye."

"Oh, we could do that, too," the captain said. "We could, couldn't we, Sergeant?"

"If you want to, sir."

"Yes, if I want to. I thought so. I don't think I want to. Too gruesome." He shuddered and dabbed at his forehead. He looked at Amos. "Now why don't you tell us about this?" He unfolded a piece of notebook paper and laid it on the table in front of him. "Your friend was carrying this when we arrested him. Unfortunately, he escaped." He dabbed at his forehead again. "You wouldn't do that, would you?"

"Oh, no, sir."

"Good. That's a good boy. It's so nice to deal with good boys." He tapped the paper with his finger. "Now what about this?"

Amos leaned over and read the paper. It was in Dunc's handwriting. "I got through, Amos," it read, "and I'm assuming you did, too. Pretty neat, huh? I'm going to have a look around. Try to meet up with me half a football field west of the monument in the middle of the plaza. If I can't meet you there, I'll leave a note. Dunc. P.S. Did you notice the pulsing light when you went through? I wonder what it means? Keep your eyes open for something valuable. Like money."

Right, Amos thought. *I should look for money. They're going to blow me away, and I should look for money.*

"What," asked the captain, "is a football field?"

"It's a field you play a game called football on," Amos answered. "You wouldn't know anything about it."

"Then why don't you explain it to me? How long is a football field?"

"One hundred y—"

"Yes?"

"Miles. One hundred miles."

The captain's eyes popped wide open.

39

"My goodness," he said, "that must be quite a game. You play that in Pennsylvania?"

"Yes, sir."

"I've never heard of it."

"It's rather new," Amos said.

"I imagine." The captain leaned over his desk and peered at Amos through his little round lenses. "You wouldn't be lying to me, now would you?"

Amos mustered up a shocked expression on his face. "No, sir."

The captain settled back in his chair. "Good. It's so nice to deal with boys who don't lie. Lying makes everything so difficult." He nodded his head at Bremish. "Prepare a party to intercept the other spy, Sergeant. Give them the fastest horses, and send them west."

"Would you like me to lead it, sir?"

"No, no, I don't think so. I'd just be lost without you here."

"Yes, sir." Sergeant Bremish saluted and left the tent.

"Now," the captain said, "why don't you tell me about these things?" He pointed to the contents of Amos's pockets, which had been emptied on the desk. Sergeant Bremish had taken them out when they had first come into the tent.

"And what is this?" the captain asked.

"It's a Superball, sir."

"A Superball? And what is a Superball?"

"It's just a ball, a toy. You bounce it. Go ahead—try it."

"You don't mind?"

"No, of course not."

The captain picked up the ball and looked at it. He looked back at Amos. "This isn't a trick, is it? It won't blow up when I drop it?"

"No, sir, it's just a ball."

"And you're not lying?"

"No, sir."

"Of course not. You're a good boy." He dropped the ball, and it bounced almost all the way back up to his hand again. "Delightful," he said. He bounced it harder, and it touched the canvas on the ceiling. He clapped his hands and smiled happily.

"You can keep it if you want, sir," Amos said.

"You don't mind? I mean, it is yours."

"I don't mind. You're going to shoot me anyway, remember?"

"Oh, that's right." He wrinkled up his face in disgust. "War is such a nasty business." He sighed. "But still, it must be done, mustn't it?" He looked back down at the desk and picked up Amos's digital wristwatch. Amos had asked for it for Christmas last year because with a push of a button it converted to a Space Zowies video game. But he had broken the wristband, so he kept it in his pocket.

"Oh, look at this!" the captain said. "There's numbers on it!"

"It's a watch, sir."

"A watch? But there are no hands. Eight forty-five. That is the right time. But—oh my goodness! It just changed to eight forty-six!"

"It's called a digital watch, sir."

"A digital watch?"

"Yes, sir, and there's more to it than that. It's also a video game."

"A video game?" The captain looked back up at Amos. "Do you play that on a football field?"

"No, sir. Let me show you." He walked around the desk and leaned over the captain's shoulder. "Now," he said, "when you push this button . . ." He pushed the mode button, and the time disappeared. Little Space Zowies started to descend toward the bottom of the screen. "And now you shoot them with this button." He pushed the fire button, and one of the Zowies disappeared in a tiny digital explosion.

"Oh, my heavens!" the captain cried. "Let me try!" He pulled the watch away from Amos's fingers and started pushing the buttons. There was another tiny digital explosion.

"I got one!"

"Good for you, sir."

"My, but this is good fun." The captain was leaning over the desk now, too absorbed in the invasion of the Space Zowies to worry about a suspected spy. Amos slipped quietly out the canvas door of the tent and disappeared into the darkness.

Chapter · 6

It was close to midnight now, and cold. Amos had been hiding in a stack of barrels near the southeast corner of the plaza for hours, waiting for the plaza to clear. There was a huge pile of boxes fifty yards west of the monument. He had been watching it for hours and had seen no movement. If Dunc was hiding there, he had hidden himself well.

The plaza was empty now except for one guard who was patrolling its perimeter. Every time he passed Amos, he walked slower and paid less attention. Amos figured three or four more rounds, and the guard would be walking in his sleep.

Amos rubbed his legs. He had been sitting cross-legged for a long time, and they were starting to get numb. He didn't try to stretch them out. A little brown spotted dog had crawled up in his lap and fallen asleep. Amos didn't mind. The little guy kept him warm.

Amos peered around the barrel directly in front of him and watched the guard. He had quit walking around the plaza and was leaning against a building on the far side. Amos watched as his head started to fall then bob back up again. He did it over and over until his head looked like a yo-yo. Finally it went down and didn't come back up. Amos waited. The guard's knees started to bend, and a moment later he slid down the wall to the ground and collapsed in a little heap. Amos woke the dog up and it yipped in complaint, then crawled out of his lap and settled itself against a barrel to sleep again. Amos stood up.

The hours of sitting had left pains like long needles in his knees, and he had to take a few minutes to rub them out. When they were gone, he looked around the plaza again. Except for the sleeping guard it was empty. He starting tiptoeing toward the monument. Halfway there, a door opened on the far side of the plaza. Yellow lamplight streamed out and framed the silhouette of Bremish as he stepped into the night.

Amos froze like a rabbit caught on the freeway in a pair of headlights, half frightened out of his wits. The sergeant stood in the doorway of the building with his hands on his hips and stared across the plaza. Evidently his eyes hadn't adjusted to the darkness yet, because he looked directly at Amos and didn't seem to see him. His moustache glowed red in the light, and the steam from his breath rose above it so his face looked like a bonfire. He hadn't seen Amos yet, but it wouldn't be long before he did.

Amos stood still a moment longer, undecided about what he should do. He looked back to the barrels he had been hiding in. Too far. He slunk silently to his right until the monument blocked his view of Bremish, then tiptoed up to it. He stuck one eye around its corner.

Bremish was still standing in the doorway with his hands on his hips, but now another man was standing there with him. "You got a light?" the other man asked.

"Yeah, McClarsky," Bremish said. "I've got a light if you've got a spare cigar."

"Sure." McClarsky reached into his pocket, took out a cigar, and gave it to Bremish. The sergeant's match lit up his face for a moment, then he handed the match to McClarsky. McClarsky lit his cigar and closed the door behind him. In the dim moonlight the glowing ends of the cigars looked like two fireflies. They danced silently around the door for a few moments, then started moving toward the monument. Amos pulled his head back and held his breath.

The two men stopped on the other side of the monument. They were so close, Amos could smell their cigars and the sweat on their bodies.

"Nice night," McClarsky said.

"Too cold," Bremish replied.

"A little." The two men were silent for a moment. "I hear the *Virginia*'s going out again tomorrow," McClarsky said. "A couple more days like the one she had today, and the blockade will be taken care of."

"Yeah."

"You're awfully quiet tonight."

"Just thinking."

"Thinking about what?"

"About those spies."

"You really think they were spies? They were just kids."

"But did you see the way they were dressed? They were dressed too strange to be just kids. And the things in the second spy's pockets. Top-secret things. He had this little sphere that he actually convinced the captain was a toy."

"I saw that sphere. It could have been a toy."

Bremish snorted. "You need to start seeing things through a trained military eye."

"And what did your trained military eye see?"

"Cannon shot. A new, special kind of

49

cannon shot. The way that thing bounced around, it could kill ten people."

"You could be right."

Bremish snorted again. "I know I'm right." He started walking around the monument with McClarsky following him. Amos had to tiptoe quickly to stay on the opposite side.

"You want to see something funny?" Bremish said.

"Sure."

"Watch this." He whistled, and Amos saw the little dog come from behind the barrels toward the monument, wagging its tail. He looked at Amos and wagged his tail harder for a moment, then went around the monument to where Bremish was standing.

"Good dog," Bremish said. "You want a piece of candy?" Amos looked around the corner. The dog was sitting up on its back legs, begging. Bremish was leaning over it. All of a sudden he jabbed his cigar against the dog's nose, and the dog ran yelping back toward the barrels. Bremish burst out in a roar of laughter.

"Why do you do things like that?" Mc-
Clarsky asked.

"It makes me feel good," Bremish said.
He puffed on his cigar. "And I'll do the same
thing to those spies if I ever catch them.
They're not the two innocent boys they
make themselves out to be. Maybe the end
of a cigar will make them tell the truth." He
took another puff, and the end of the cigar
glowed red. All of the sudden he took the
cigar out of his mouth and stared across the
plaza.

"Where's that guard?" he said.

"I don't know."

"Guard!"

Amos heard a snuffling and snorting
from where the guard had fallen asleep.
Luckily, the guard was on the same side of
the monument as Bremish and McClarsky.

"Yes, Sergeant?" the guard asked. Amos
could hear the sleep in his voice.

"What are you doing over there?"

"I thought I heard something," the guard
lied.

"Oh?" Bremish said. "Could it be one of
the spies?"

"Yeah, that's it!" the guard said. "It could be one of the spies!"

"Let's go," Bremish told McClarsky. The two men started walking toward the guard. As soon as they left, Amos slunk like a shadow toward the boxes, where he hoped Dunc would be waiting.

Amos was hiding in the boxes by the time Bremish and McClarsky got back to the monument. The guard was with them. Amos looked around. There was no one else hiding with him.

"Nothing," Bremish growled.

"I swear, I know I heard something," the guard lied again.

"Maybe it was a rat," McClarsky suggested.

"Yeah, maybe." Bremish threw his cigar on the ground. "Keep your eyes open, guard."

"Yes, Sergeant."

"It's cold out here," Bremish said. "Come on, McClarsky. Let's go back inside." He led the smaller man back toward the door they had come out of. There was a splash of light when the door opened, and Amos had to duck behind a box. When the door closed, it was dark again.

The guard resumed his patrol around the plaza. Amos waited. It only took two trips before he was leaning against the wall and sound asleep again.

Amos started quietly searching through the boxes. He couldn't tell what was in them, but they were big and heavy, and Amos assumed they were filled with ammunition. He thought for a moment that maybe Bremish had hidden gold in them, but no one in the whole world could own that much gold. After a few minutes he found a note tucked between two slats of a wooden box on the side of the pile farthest away from the monument. It was almost too dark to read it in the moonlight.

"Sorry I couldn't make it," the note read. "I have to hide from Bremish. Look out for him. He's a big man, and I think he's really dangerous. He's a sergeant in the Army and pure mean." Amos looked up. He thought he heard a noise, but it was just the guard snoring. "I think I've figured out the pulses," Dunc continued. "I think they have something to do with either how many people have gone through or how many more people can go through, you know what I mean? I saw three when I went through. How many did you see? Forget about the cannons for your paper. Do it on the battle between the *Monitor* and the *Merrimack*. It happens tomorrow. Go down by the docks. I'll be waiting for you there. If we don't see each other, just go through the portal after the battle and I'll see you back home. I'm sure you remember the directions and the code word. Dunc."

"Directions?" Amos said out loud, almost too loud. "Dunc, you know how I am with directions. And the code word was . . . was . . . well, it was g-a-z-something. You can tell me tomorrow." He peeked over the boxes at the guard. He was still asleep. Amos stood up and crept across the plaza in the direction that he thought led to the docks. He had to find Dunc.

Chapter·7

"This," the man said in a voice that sounded like gravel being swished around in a bucket, "is an historic day. This is a day for celebration!"

Amos looked at the man. He had a long black moustache that curled up to tickle each side of his nose and a big smile on his face. He looked like he wanted to celebrate. Amos didn't feel like celebrating. After spending the night sleeping on a coil of rope under a smelly horse blanket to try to keep warm, no one would feel like celebrating.

The man climbed on top of a crate and

raised his hands to quiet the tittering of the crowd. "Ladies and gentlemen, please!" The crowd quieted itself down. Some of the women had parasols and closed them so the people behind them could see better. Others looked at Amos and whispered among themselves before they turned to face the man. *It's because I'm ugly,* he thought, *and my mother dresses me funny.*

The man raised his hands again and then dropped them to his sides. "You are here to witness an historic event," he said. The crowd started tittering again, and a few of the more enthusiastic members started to clap and cheer.

"An historic event," the man repeated, "that will change the course of the war!" Now there was a general round of applause. A few members of a brass band that waited impatiently off to one side started playing "Dixie," but the band conductor cut them off.

"An historic event," the man said for the third time, "that will break this blockade that is choking the life out of your sons and daughters, that is choking the life out of our very city, that is choking the life out of our dear Confederacy!" The applause was louder and Amos joined in, partly so he would not look too conspicuous and partly because he was getting caught up in the fervor of it all.

"And this grand ship," the man said, motioning with his arm, "is what is going to do it!" Everyone was cheering now, and try as he might, the conductor couldn't keep the band from breaking out in an impromptu run of "Dixie." The crowd started singing the words, and Amos cheered just because he didn't know what else to do.

He looked through his clapping hands at the ship. It was a strange-looking vessel, all flat and metal and low, with what looked like a huge iron pup tent staked out on its deck and barrels of cannons peering out of the tent like open-mouthed Cub Scouts. It was the *Merrimack,* or as the southerners preferred, the *Virginia.* Today was the day that they thought it would sail out into the harbor and break the blockade. Today was the day it would actually sail out into the harbor and come back after fighting the

Monitor, no worse for the battle but with the blockade still intact. All the cheering was for nothing. Amos stopped cheering, not only because the historic day the gravel-voiced man had been promising wouldn't happen, but also because it suddenly occurred to him that Dunc had promised to be here but was nowhere to be seen.

A steam whistle on the ship tooted once, and the crowd went wild as the ship started to pull slowly away from the pier. Amos searched frantically for Dunc but found him nowhere. As he searched, he saw a big man in front of him with a parrot on his shoulder. The parrot turned around and looked at Amos, belched, and went to the bathroom all down the back of the man's coat. The man said a word that Amos had once thought of but had never used—even when he got his thumb caught in the spokes of his bicycle—and the bird said, "Treasure map." Amos stopped searching for a moment and looked at the bird. It looked so familiar. . . .

The ship tooted again, and Amos realized he didn't have time to try and figure out how he remembered the parrot. He began searching again. As he looked, a pretty girl with long dark hair flowing out from beneath a pink bonnet turned her head to look at him. She smiled. Right at him. Amos froze.

The girl was Melissa.

Chapter · 8

Melissa smiled at him again and leaned her head toward another girl who was standing next to her. She watched him with big blue eyes, and even through the crowd Amos could hear her speak.

"Look at that strange-looking boy over there," she said. "Isn't he ever so cute?" The other girl looked, and together they giggled. Amos reached down to pick his jaw up off the ground.

"She must have been looking for me when I went through the hole," he whispered to himself. "She must have seen how I did it and gone through after me. She must really love me if she's willing to travel through time to be with me." Melissa waved, and he raised his hand to wave back. His hand was shaking so hard, he didn't have to wave it. It waved itself. *All these years, all this time she's loved me.*

"Be cool now," he said to himself, "just be cool. They like it when you're cool." He lowered his hand and put on his cool expression. Melissa looked at him and said something to her friend that he didn't hear.

"All right, you're cool," he said, as if he were trying to convince himself. "Now go over and talk to her." He didn't know what he would say. He had never spoken to her before, and Melissa had only said six words to him in his whole life. He had been standing next to her in the lunch line at school, and she had turned to him and said, "Hey, you're standing on my foot."

Now Amos's shoes were untied, and when he tried to take a step forward, he found that he was standing on his shoelaces. He started falling down. *Great,* he had time to think—*she finally loves me, and*

I'm going to make a complete dork out of myself.

He fell forward into an elderly woman who shrieked and started beating him with her parasol. He took a step back and raised his arms to fend off the blows. He took another step back, and on the third step back his heel caught on a mooring line, and he fell off the pier head over heels into the water.

Dork, he thought—*classic dork.* Just before his head went under, he saw, upside down, the aft part of the *Merrimack.* There was a white piece of notebook paper wedged between two plates of armor.

The water was cold. He came up sputtering, with dirt and mud running from his hair into his eyes. Two overhand reaches brought him to the *Merrimack.* As he reached for the gunwale, strong hands grabbed his shoulders and started to pull him up. He clawed the paper note and shoved it into his pocket before they had him on the deck.

"You all right, son?" A sailor with sunburned skin and creases around his eyes was looking at him.

"Yeah, I'm fine. I just tripped."

"I'll say you did." The ship had stopped and was slowly backing up toward the pier. Amos looked at the sailor, then at the people in the crowd. Some where laughing, and some looked concerned. Melissa looked concerned.

"Where'd you get these funny clothes, son?" the sailor asked.

"I got them . . . my mom made them."

"She's not much for making clothes, is she?" They were at the pier now, and the sailor helped him off the ship. "Tell your mom to get you some dry, less funny clothes," he said.

"I will."

"Good." The sailor waved toward the iron tent, and the boat started back out to the bay. The crowd cheered again, and the band started playing.

Amos stood shivering and watched the *Merrimack* move away from the pier. He remembered the note and reached into his pocket. He felt a hand on his shoulder. When he turned around he saw Melissa.

"Land sakes," Melissa said, "are you all right?"

"Fine. A little cold." He stood there shivering and watched a puddle form around his feet. "Melissa, why did you follow me?"

"Follow you?" She looked puzzled.

"Do you know where the time hole is? I can't remember. If you do, we've got to find Dunc and—"

"You are a strange boy, aren't you? I just don't know what you are talking about."

"Melissa, we don't have time for this. We—"

"Melissa? Who is this Melissa?"

"Aren't you Melissa?"

"I think that cold water has addled your brain. There's no Melissa here. My name's Maggie."

"Maggie? You're not Melissa?"

"My name is Maggie Hansen, and I've never heard of a Melissa. What's your name?"

"Amos. Amos Binder."

"Well, Amos Binder," she said, "you are a
very strange boy, and you're going to be a
very sick boy if we don't get you home and
out of these wet clothes."

"You can't take me home."

"And why not?"

"It's a long story. I live a long way from
here."

"Then we'll take you to my house." She
held him by the arm and started leading
him off the pier. "You can borrow some of
my brother's clothes until yours are dry."
Amos let her lead him. *I've dreamt of this
all my life,* he thought. *She loves me. She
really loves me. Dunc will never believe
this. . . .*

He took his hand out of his pocket but
left the note inside.

Maggie led him down the waterfront and
up a street leading away from the bay toward a long row of large, stately mansions.
The air was cold, and the water had soaked
to his skin, and he was shivering violently.

"Don't worry," she said, "it won't be
long." She squeezed his arm tight and
started to hug it to her side, but backed off a

second later. "You're so wet," she said, "I can't even hug you. And you're such a cute boy."

Amos didn't say anything. He was never very good at accepting compliments—probably because he didn't get very many—and he'd never had any experience accepting them from Melissa Hansen, or even from girls who looked like Melissa Hansen, for that matter.

"So," she said, "you're not from around here?"

"No," Amos said. He thought for a moment. "Yes."

"No or yes? Which is it?"

"No and yes. I mean, I don't live here, but I spend a lot of time here, I guess."

"Oh?"

"Yeah. With an uncle."

"Do I know him?"

"Probably not."

"What's his name?"

Amos thought quickly. "Bremish. Sergeant Bremish. He's in the Army."

"I don't know him."

"That's good." He said it out loud, but his

teeth-chattering distorted it too much for her to understand.

"Well, here we are," Maggie said. She swung him around and headed him up a walk to a large white house with green shutters. "Mummy will be so glad to see you. Mummy simply loves helping people. And she loves funny stories. She'll love to hear about the cute boy in the funny clothes who fell off the pier. And she'll tell everyone in town. The whole town will be talking about you."

"Great, that's just great," he said, not too enthusiastically. *I am the dork,* he thought, *and everybody will talk about me. Super dork.* She opened the door and led him inside.

Amos found himself standing in an elegant foyer with a brass chandelier overhead and an ornate mirror on the wall. He looked in the mirror and saw how shabby he looked. He felt like a half-drowned rat waiting at the entrance to Buckingham Palace to see the queen.

"Now you wait here," Maggie said, "and I'll go fetch you some dry clothes, then we'll sit down and have lunch and make a party of it. It will be such fun! Mummy!" She left the foyer and disappeared around a corner.

As soon as he was alone, Amos reached into his pocket and took out the note. It was soaking wet and began to tear as he tried to unfold it. When he finally did get it unfolded, it was in three pieces, and most of the ink had run so badly, he couldn't read it. ". . . quickly . . . time . . . trapped here . . . going through . . . directions for portal . . . next note at plaza . . . Bremish watching . . ." was all he could make out. He put the note back in his pocket and debated if having lunch with a girl who looked just like Melissa was worth the risk of missing the hole.

The decision wasn't easy—Maggie was such a perfect copy of Melissa, and he had waited so long—but before Maggie came back with the clothes, he had left the house and was running, his shoes squelching with every step, back toward the plaza.

Love was great, but being a hundred and thirty years in the past wouldn't work. They didn't have anything he liked—except Maggie. No hamburgers, no video games, no tennis shoes, no skateboards, no sidewalks, no television. Well, that wasn't so bad. But no anything else. And of course, no Dunc.

Chapter·9

He was so cold when he reached the plaza, his knees would hardly bend. He lurched forward like Frankenstein in an old horror movie. The plaza was alive with people, people everywhere, running about as if there were a war going on, and it took him a moment to remember that there was.

"The note," he said to himself, "I've got to find the note." He began to look around. There were so many people there, he couldn't see anything but legs and bodies and faces. And cannons. There were three long lines of cannons, more than fifty of them.

Amos worked his way through the people over to the south side of the plaza and collapsed against a wall in the southwest corner. It was impossible. He was going to have to stay, locked in the past, if he didn't find the note, and he couldn't think, couldn't think. . . .

He looked at all the people and all the cannons and buried his head in his hands in frustration. It was hopeless. There was no possible way to find a single sheet of notebook paper in all this chaos.

He was stuck in the Civil War until the day he died—which, if Sergeant Bremish had his way, would not be very far away and would not be very pleasant. He heard swearing and looked up to see Sergeant Bremish nearby. *I should surrender,* he thought—*it would be better to die right away than prolong the suffering*. He was so cold, his teeth felt brittle. What was the difference—a world without video games and hamburgers was not a world worth living in.

The people began to move out of the way as team after team of horses were brought in to haul away the cannons. Amos watched the men hook up the horses' harnesses to the cannon frames and drive them away, bumping and clattering and clanking. Cannon after cannon left the plaza, and soon the large yard began to look empty.

Two men were hooking up a cannon right in front of him. He listened as they spoke.

"Why are we moving everything out?" one of them asked. He was only a boy, just a few years older than Amos.

"We have to get them out of here," an older man said. "The Yankees have their own armored ship. The *Virginia* can't get past it."

"So?"

"So it looks like the blockade is going to hold. We have to get these cannons to General Lee before everything collapses and the Yankees get hold of them."

One of the horses in the team, a big mottled gray, whinnied loudly and tried to jump out of its harness. "Whoa, girl," the man said.

"What's spooking her?" the boy asked.

"I don't know. Must be the excitement of it all. Let's get this cannon out of here." They finished hooking up the harness and motioned to the driver to leave. Amos watched the team as it left. The driver was going through the plaza fast—too fast—and as he rounded a pile of crates, the gray mare almost stepped on the brown spotted dog that was rummaging in the boxes. She spooked and jumped into the air. The cannon careened to the side, and the right wheel bounced up into the crates. There was a sharp crack like thunder as the wooden spokes broke and the wheel snapped in half. The cannon skidded to a halt.

The man and the boy ran across the plaza toward the broken cannon. "We'll just pull it over to the side," the man shouted. "I'll find a wheelwright to fix it later. Let's get the rest of them out of here."

Amos sat where he was and watched them working. There was something about the cannon—something about it, like the parrot, that was very familiar. . . .

He could swear he had seen that cannon before, somewhere in the past . . .

Or somewhere in the future.

Chapter · 10

Amos was on his feet and running toward the broken cannon before he knew what he was doing. It was the cannon, the courthouse cannon, and the mystery of the note he and Dunc had found in its barrel suddenly made sense to him.

The *D* on the note was short for *Dunc,* and Bremish wasn't after them because they stole something from him—he was after them because he thought they were spies.

And Amos had only one chance. Just one chance to go back through and get home. He ran toward the cannon, and the men that were working on it, as fast as he could. He had to see the note. He couldn't remember which corner of the plaza the time hole was in, and he couldn't remember the code word. He knew it was g-something. He knew it was g-a-z-something.

The man and the boy were frantically trying to move the cannon to the north side of the plaza, out of the way. They weren't having much luck. The gray mare was still frightened and was pulling in the direction opposite from the way the other horse was trying to go. The boy was trying to calm the mare while the man was pushing against the broken wheel.

"What's going on here?"

Amos froze where he stood. It was Bremish's voice.

"What's going on here?" the voice repeated. Amos saw the sergeant striding across the plaza toward the broken cannon. Bremish hadn't seen him yet.

"The wheel broke," the boy said. "We're just trying to get the cannon out of the way."

"Well, put some muscle into it," Bremish said. He had reached the cannon now, and he motioned the man pushing on the wheel out of the way. With a mighty heave he pushed the cannon against the wall.

"There now," Bremish said, brushing the dirt off of his hands, "all it takes is a little grit, and you can do wonders. Now get this team unhooked, and get back to the other cannons. I—" He stopped in midsentence. He had turned around and seen Amos standing in the middle of the courtyard.

"You!" Bremish shouted. "Come here!" He started moving toward Amos.

"Come here!" Bremish shouted again. He was getting closer now. Amos tried to calculate if he could work his way around Bremish and reach the cannon. He thought he could until the sergeant pulled a revolver out of his side holster and pointed it at him. *It's time,* Amos thought—*time to run.*

"Stop!" Bremish yelled. "Stop or I'll shoot!"

That's where that line comes from, Amos thought, his legs pounding. He'd heard that

79

line in every cop show on television: *Stop or I'll shoot.* Bremish had started it.

Amos didn't listen to him. He barreled toward the northwest corner of the plaza.

There were still enough horses and people milling about that Amos had to do some fancy dodging to reach the corner. When he got there, he stood still for a moment. He couldn't remember the code word. He knew it was g-a-z-something.

"Gazelle!" he shouted. Nothing happened. He looked over his shoulder. Sergeant Bremish was getting closer.

"Gazette!" Nothing happened again.

"Don't move, spy! If you move, I'll shoot!"

"Gaz—gaz . . ." Amos threw up his hands. *Work, brain, before he shoots us. Come on!* Bremish was almost on him, and he couldn't wait any longer. He started running toward the northeast corner.

Amos heard a shot, and a bullet spanged off the wall beside him. He didn't stop. He ran faster.

"Stop!" Bremish bellowed.

When he reached the northeast corner, he was so out of breath, he almost couldn't say what he thought might be the code word. "Gazelle!" he whispered breathlessly.

Nothing happened.

"Gazette?"

Nothing happened again. Bremish was almost on him, and he took off for the southeast corner.

"Stop him!" Bremish yelled. "Somebody grab him!"

Amos was dodging around traffic so fast, he lost his sense of direction. When he got to the south side, he realized he was closer to the southwest corner than he was to the southeast, so he took off in that direction, shouting as he went.

"Gazelle!"

Again nothing happened. Amos looked at the corner ahead of him. The brown spotted dog was hiding there, watching him.

"Gazette!"

Nothing happened again. Amos was getting tired now, and his wet clothes were slowing him down. Bremish was so close, Amos could almost feel his breath.

"Gaz . . . gaz . . ." He just couldn't think of the word—try as he might, he just couldn't think of it. He felt Bremish's fingertips brush the back of his neck.

"Gazebo!" he shouted. "The word's *gazebo*!"

An outline of a door appeared on the wall directly in front of him. It glowed brightly with yellow light. The dog sniffed and took a step toward it.

"No!" Amos shouted. The dog looked over its shoulder at him for a second, then took another step. The door was still there, so close, and the dog stuck his nose into it.

"Got you!" Amos felt his collar pull tight across the front of his neck as Bremish grabbed his sweatshirt. *The dog will go through,* he thought—*a dog will come walking out of the dressing room, and I'll be stuck here with Bremish.*

He was almost to the door now. A strangled cry escaped his throat, and as he tried to wriggle loose, he stepped on his shoelaces again. His collar tore free of Bremish's grasp, and he fell forward in a perfect swan dive. The dog saw him flying through the air overhead, and it leaped out of the way.

Amos was engulfed in a world of searing yellow light. He felt dizzy.

When his head cleared, he found himself in a little room. There were mirrors on the walls and sweaters on the floor, and he found himself looking at his own reflection —a dripping wet, soggy Amos with mud in his hair.

He was back.

Chapter · 11

He was dizzy for a moment and had to sit down on the floor to keep from falling. As he rested, someone tossed a sweater over the door, and it landed on his head.

"Hey!"

"Amos, is that you?" It was Dunc.

"Yeah, it's me."

"You made it! What took you so long?"

"What took me so long?"

"Yeah."

"I'm chased around by a man the size of a small mountain range and almost get trapped in time, and the first question out of your mouth is what took me so long?"

"Well, yeah. I've been waiting for you." Another sweater came over the top of the door.

"Hey!"

"What?"

"Will you quit throwing sweaters on me?"

"I have to. Ramone is getting suspicious. He keeps asking what's taking you so long."

"And what are you telling him?"

"That you haven't found the color you want."

Amos stood up and shook his head. The dizziness was gone. "Well, I'm done trying on sweaters." He opened the door, and Dunc came in and shut the door behind him.

"You look terrible," Dunc said. "How'd you get so wet?"

"It's a long story."

"It turned out kind of funny, didn't it? I ended up writing the note that sent us back there in the first place."

"Yeah, hilarious." He bent over and put his hands on his knees. His back ached.

How did that happen? So did his shoulders. It must have been from falling in the water. And he was still soaked.

"Let's try it again." Dunc said. "I figured it out. We could never have met. I was a few minutes ahead of you in time, so we could never be in the same place. But if we try it again and go through holding hands, we'll come out in the same time—"

"Are you completely crazy?"

"Just to see if it still works. It only pulsed once when I came back through. How many times did it pulse when you came back?"

"It didn't pulse at all."

"That's what I thought. It pulses one time less every time someone uses it. It should be all used up now."

"Well, I don't want to find out."

"We have to. We have to know if anyone else can go through."

"Why?"

"What if Bremish heard the code word?"

"You've got a point." Amos tried to imagine Bremish in the dressing room. With a gun. He took Dunc's hand.

"Give it a try."

Amos took a deep breath. "Gazelle," he said.

"Wrong word."

"Oh, yeah. I found that out with Bremish breathing down my neck. Gazebo."

Nothing happened.

"Let me try," Dunc said. "Gazebo."

Nothing happened again.

Dunc scratched his head. "Well, it looks like it's all used up. The end of an adventure. Kind of sad, isn't it?"

"Oh, yeah. I'll be crying all night on this one." Amos looked down at the sweaters lying on the floor. "What do we do with all of these?"

"Pick one out. Buy it for your mom or something."

"Why for my mom? What about Melissa?"

"She was just here. When she asked why I was in a women's clothing store, I said I was waiting for you."

"What else did you say?"

"I told her you were trying on some women's sweaters."

"And?"

"And what?"

"You must have told her more than that! You'd *better* have told her more than that!"

"She didn't give me the chance. She started laughing and left."

Amos collapsed down to the floor again. "Great," he said, "just great. Now she'll never talk to me."

Dunc changed the subject. "Did you get enough information for your paper?" he asked.

"Yeah, I guess so. I was on the *Merrimack*."

"Really? Me too."

"I know. I found your note." He picked up an extra fluffy sweater and started drying his hair. "And I met Melissa's great-great-grandmother. Her name is—was—Maggie."

"How do you know she was an ancestor of Melissa's?"

"She had to be. She looked just like her."

"That doesn't necessarily mean she was Melissa's great-great-great grandmother."

"Yeah, I guess you're right." He stood up. "Actually, when I think of it, there's no possible way she could have been Melissa's great-grandmother."

"Why not?"

"Because they were far too different to be related," Amos said. "Maggie liked me."

Amos sloshed through the store toward the exit. When they reached the sales counter, Amos put the sweater that he had dried his hair with down next to the cash register. Ramone stared down at him. He touched the sweater the way he might touch a snake.

"What on earth . . ."

"Don't ask," Amos said. "Please, don't ask."

"But it's wet—you're wet . . ."

"He's had a rough day," Dunc said. "I'll take him home now."

"Yes," Amos said. "Take me home now."

And Dunc led Amos out of the store and the mall and down the street.